A NOTE TO PARENTS

 P9-DNC-816

Reading Aloud with Your Child

Research shows that reading books aloud is the single most valuable support parents can provide in helping children learn to read.

- Be a ham! The more enthusiasm you display, the more your child will enjoy the book.
- Run your finger underneath the words as you read to signal that the print carries the story.
- Leave time for examining the illustrations more closely; encourage your child to find things in the pictures.
- Invite your youngster to join in whenever there's a repeated phrase in the text.
- Link up events in the book with similar events in your child's life.
- If your child asks a question, stop and answer it. The book can be a means to learning more about your child's thoughts.

Listening to Your Child Read Aloud

The support of your attention and praise is absolutely crucial to your child's continuing efforts to learn to read.

- If your child is learning to read and asks for a word, give it immediately so that the meaning of the story is not interrupted. DO NOT ask your child to sound out the word.
- On the other hand, if your child initiates the act of sounding out, don't intervene.
- If your child is reading along and makes what is called a miscue, listen for the sense of the miscue. If the word "road" is substituted for the word "street," for instance, no meaning is lost. Don't stop the reading for a correction.
- If the miscue makes no sense (for example, "horse" for "house"), ask your child to reread the sentence because you're not sure you understand what's just been read.
- Above all else, enjoy your child's growing command of print and make sure you give lots of praise. *You are your child's first teacher — and the most important one. Praise from you is critical for further risk-taking and learning.*

— Priscilla Lynch
   Ph.D., New York University
   Educational Consultant

To Shiny, Willy, Milly, Tilly, and Henry

Library of Congress Cataloging-in-Publication Data

Brewster, Patience.
    Too many puppies : by Patience Brewster.
        p.   cm.— (Hello reader! Level 2)
        Summary: A little girl looks forward to keeping all of Milly's puppies, but when
    they begin to make big demands on her, she changes her mind about them.
        ISBN 0-590-60276-4
        [1. Dogs—Fiction. 2. Animals—Infancy—Fiction] I. Title. II. Series.
    PZ7.B7572To   1997
    [E]—dc20   96-7402
                                                                    CIP
                                                                    AC

12 11 10 9 8 7 6 5 4 3 2 1   7 8 9/9 0 1 2/0

Printed in the U.S.A.   24

First Scholastic printing, February 1997

Too Many Puppies

by Patience Brewster

Hello Reader! — Level 2

SCHOLASTIC INC.

New York Toronto London Auckland Sydney

Milly is getting fat.
She is having puppies.

I can't wait.
It won't be long.
I can feel the puppies
kicking in Millie's tummy.

I can't wait to have
so many puppies.
Mommy says she has homes
for all the puppies.
We will only have them
while they are small.
I want to keep all the puppies.
Mommy says that would be
too many puppies.

While I sleep one night,
Milly has seven tiny puppies.
They cannot even open their eyes.
I've never seen puppies so small.
I love, love, **love** these puppies.

I tell Mommy I have to keep them all.
Says Mommy, "That would be
too many puppies."

The puppies grow fast.
They are fuzzier now.
They are trying to open their eyes.
The puppies are very
hungry and sleepy.

Milly is a good mommy.
She feeds them and
keeps them clean.

I watch them all day because
I'm keeping all the puppies.
"No way," says Mommy.
"That would be too many puppies."

Now the puppies
are fluffy and fat.
Their eyes are open.

I give each puppy a name.
There's Fatty, Floppy,
Flower, Scaredy, Happy,
Shiny, and George.

They yip and yap.
They roll and flop.

Milly loves the puppies.
I love the puppies.

Mommy loves the puppies.
I'm keeping all the puppies!

Now these puppies are really big! I help feed them now so Milly can take a rest.

I also have to help clean up after them.
They are too much work for Milly.
I can tell Milly thinks
maybe she has too many puppies!
Not me! I don't mind helping.
I am keeping all these puppies.

Yikes, now these puppies bark loudly,
and they make a mess!
It seems as if I am always
cleaning up after them.

They are always hungry.
Milly doesn't feed the puppies anymore.
They are too big.

It seems as if I'm feeding them
every minute.

These puppies are a lot of work.
They all pile on top of me
when I feed them
or when I want to play
with just one puppy.

It's time to take the puppies to the vet.
It takes a long time to get
one, two, three, four,
five, six, seven puppies
into the car.
And then one, two, three,
four, five, six, seven puppies
into the vet's office,
and back into the car,
and back home.
Mommy and Milly are right!
We have **too many puppies!**

Today the people come for their puppies.

I give each person a perfect puppy.
The people are so happy
and each puppy is so happy
to have its very own family
to play with.

There are a lot of
puppy kisses today.

At first I feel sad.

Then I remember the day
I got Milly.

I hug her. I tell her,
"Seven puppies were really, really, really fun.
But, one puppy…

one grown-up, wonderful puppy…
is just right!"